Walt Disney's

DUMBO

Dearmurtaza.

FROM ARjun
Happy birthday

MP: for Noe
AM: for Callum and Ewan

Paperback edition: ISBN: 1-84248-080-4
Hardback edition: ISBN: 1-84248-081-2

Paperback edition first published 2003 by Mathew Price Ltd.
Hardback edition first published 2003 by Mathew Price Ltd.
The Old Glove Factory, Bristol Road, Sherborne, Dorset DT9 4HP

Printed in China by Imago

WALT DISNEY'S
DUMBO

WRITTEN BY MATHEW PRICE

ILLUSTRATED BY ATSUKO MOROZUMI

MATHEW PRICE LIMITED

I'll never forget when Dumbo was born. The circus was travelling from town to town, giving shows, and Dumbo was actually born on the train.

Oh, who am I? Timothy Q. Mouse,
at your service.

He was so adorable,
we all thought so.

It wasn't till he
sneezed and his
ears flew open that
we realised how
big they were. They
were extraordinary.

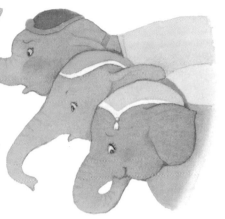

The other elephants were not kind. His real name was Jumbo Junior,
but they called him Dumbo, and it stuck.

His mother never cared. She just loved him.
And everything was fine and dandy, till we reached the next stop.

Of course, there was a parade, and Dumbo wanted to join in, naturally.

But, oh, those ears!
He couldn't take two steps
without tripping over them.

Trouble was, some of the local kids
started to tease him. They were just bullies, nothing else.

Boy, his mummy didn't like that! She gave one of them a good spanking, and then there was trouble.

If you ask me the boy deserved it, but the Ringmaster called her a rogue elephant and started cracking his whip and scaring her half to death. "Capture her!" he shouted, and she was shackled and dragged away.

They stuck her in a jail for mad elephants. Dumbo was brokenhearted.

You'd think those other elephants would comfort him, but not a bit.

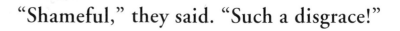

"Shameful," they said. "Such a disgrace!"

The Ringmaster
had plans for Dumbo.
He wanted to build a
pyramid of elephants
and then springboard
him to the top.
Great idea!

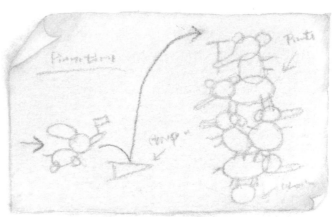

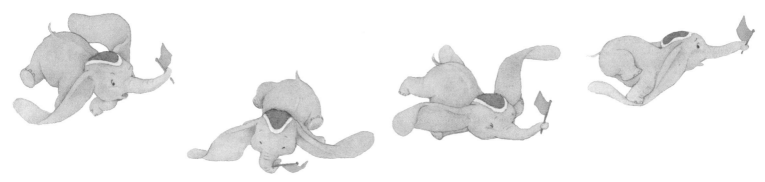

But those ears!
Whenever he ran, he tripped over them. I was at my wit's end.

Finally I tied them up over his head and hoped for the best.

For the first few strides Dumbo was fine, but then his ears came undone, he tripped...

...and tumbled headlong into the other elephants.
The whole precarious pyramid came crashing down.

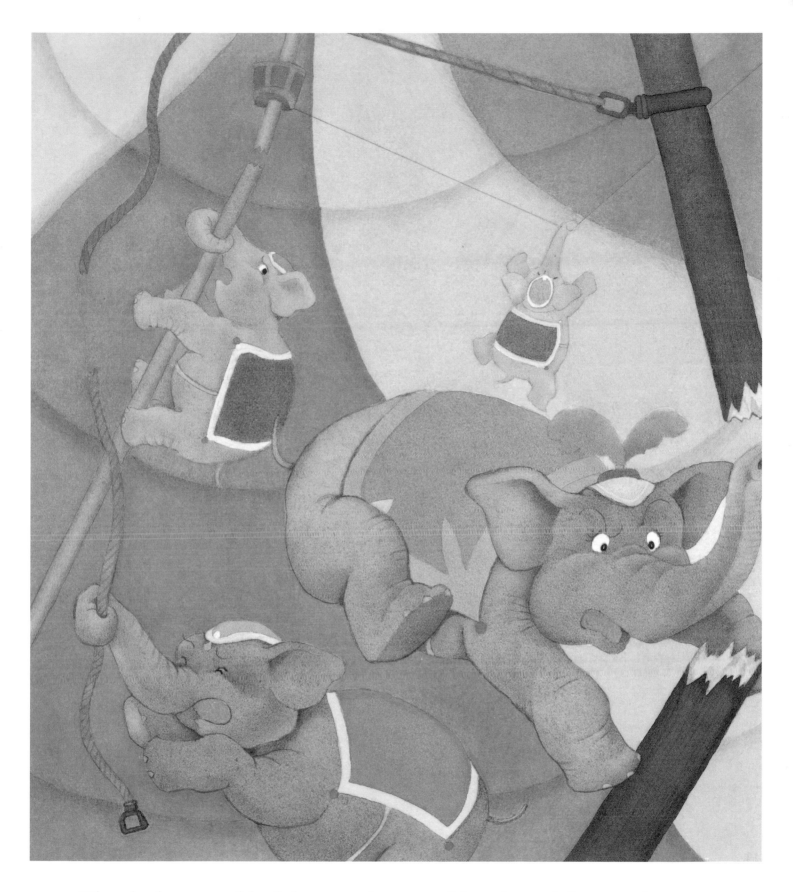

The elephants grabbed desperately at anything that might save them. Ropes snapped, tent poles splintered and broke, and with a terrible cracking, tearing sound, the big top collapsed.

After that the other elephants wouldn't speak to Dumbo.

Then the circus made him a clown, and the other clowns threw pies in his face.

They made him leap off the top of a
burning tower. The audience loved it.
"Bravo!" they shouted. "Encore!"

For the clowns, this new act was a huge success. They couldn't wait
to celebrate.
"Hey, if the people like it that much when he jumps from thirty feet,"
one said, "they'll like it twice as much if he jumps from
three hundred."
"Let's make it a thousand!" said another.
I'd had enough.
"Hey, Dumbo. How'd you like to go and see your mummy?"

And, just for a little while,
Dumbo and his mummy
were together again,
till it was time
to get back.

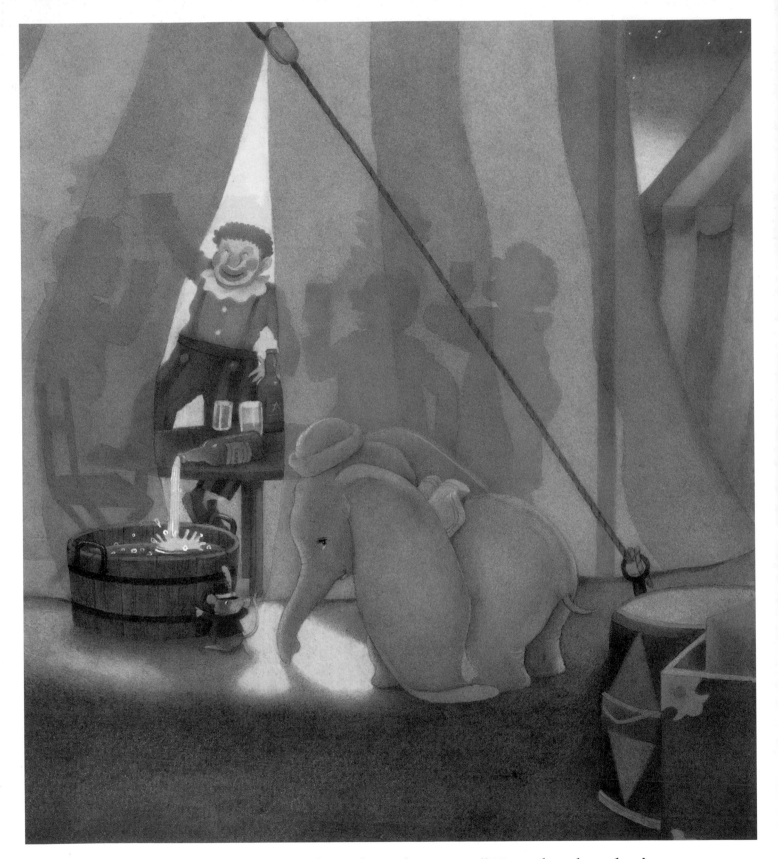

As we walked back, I tried to cheer him up. "Hey, dumbo, don't cry.
You're a success. Besides, crying only gives you hiccups."
"Hic!"
"There, what did I tell you? Here, have a drink."

"That's it, have a good long drink.

"What's the matter? You look funny.

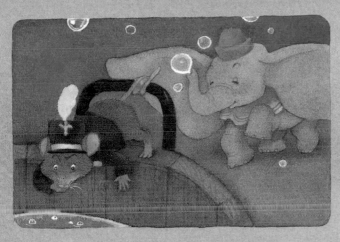

"Oh, oh, What's in that water?"

"Oops!

"Hic! Bubbles, It's bubbly."

As I climbed out, I remember Dumbo
was looking silly, but I don't remember
anything after that.

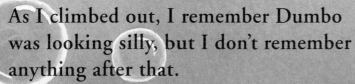

I woke up to find a bunch of crows looking at me.

"Wake up, rat," they said.

"Go away," I said. "What are you birds doing down here anyway?
Why don't you fly up a tree where you belong?"

"*Down* here? Well, hear him talk. Look around you Baby Rat."

"Listen, I ain't a baby and I ain't no rat–"

"And I suppose you and no elephant ain't up in no tree, neither?"

"No!...

...Tree?...

...DUMBO! DON'T
LOOK DOWN!"

"Help!"

"Ooh!"

"Ouch!"

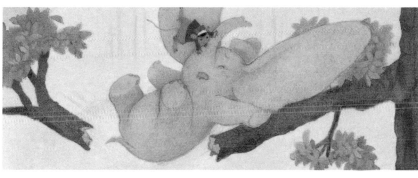

"Aaah!"

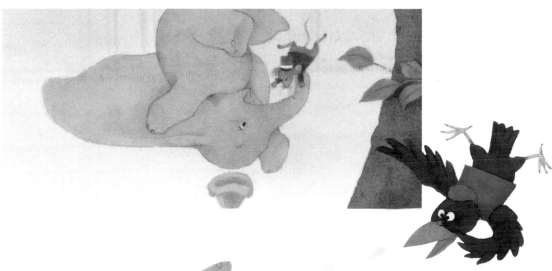

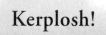

Kerplosh!

I just couldn't figure it out.
"How did we get up there in the first place?"
I said to myself. "Climbed up? Nah.
Elephants can't climb trees. Jumped?
Nah – too high."

"Hey, maybe you flew up."

"Flew up? Yeah, maybe we flew up."

"THAT'S IT!
Dumbo, you flew. Boy, am I stupid!
Your ears! Just look at them! They're perfect wings!"

Those crows just laughed and laughed and laughed.

"Did *you* ever see an elephant fly?"

"I've seen a horsefly!"

"I've seen a housefly!"

"I've seen a dragonfly!"

That did it.

"All right." I said. "This has gone far enough. You ought to be ashamed of yourselves. A bunch of big guys like you picking on a poor little elephant like him. Suppose you were torn away from your mother when you were just a baby? Suppose everybody said you were a freak because of your big ears? Suppose... ah, but what's the use of talking to you coldhearted birds?

"Come on, Dumbo."

But really, those birds were all right. Anyway, they came after us. "Hold on, now," they said. "Don't go away feeling like that.

"Now, you want to make the elephant fly, you got to use a little collegey – you know, psychology!

"You get yourself a magic feather – catch on?"
"That's not a magic feather …

"Oh, a magic feather You mean …
Yeah, I gotcha.

"Hey, Dumbo! Have I got it! The magic feather. Now you can fly!"

Somehow, I just knew
Dumbo could fly.
"Go on, Dumbo,
flap those ears.
Up down, up down.
Faster, faster."

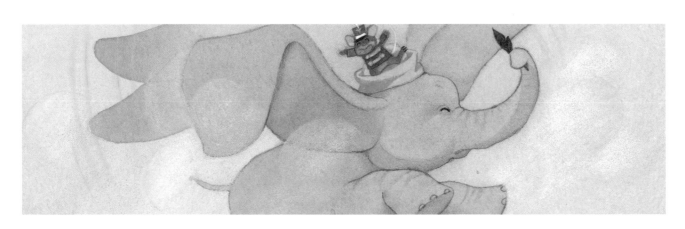

Then, just when I was giving up – HOT DIGGITY!

"Dumbo! You're flying!"

Dumbo was a natural-born flier.
Those circus folks were in for a big surprise.

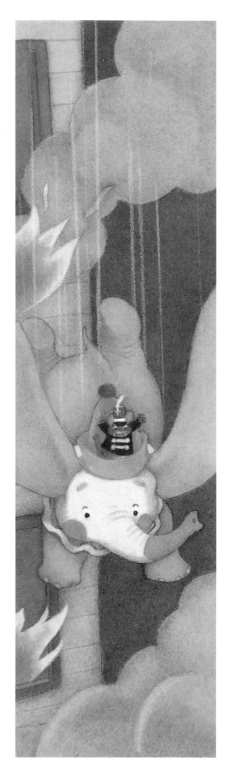

The big night came,
"Got your magic
feather?" I said.
"Then let's go."

Dumbo jumped.
Halfway down, the
feather slipped out
of his trunk.

I was terrified.
We were going faster
and faster.

I shouldn't have worried. Dumbo pulled out of a perfect dive, and we were making history.

We gave them loop-the-loop,

the low glide,

and a few party tricks, too...

Serve 'em right!

The crowd loved it. Couldn't get enough of us.

Of course, we were famous overnight. Everybody wanted us.
We went to Hollywood.

The circus even gave Dumbo his own carriage.

THE
END